NO LONGER PROPERTY OF
SEATTLE PUBLIC LIBRARY

P9-DUD-559

Splotch

by Gianna Marino

viking

Before school.

Bye, Splotch. See you after school.

Noon.

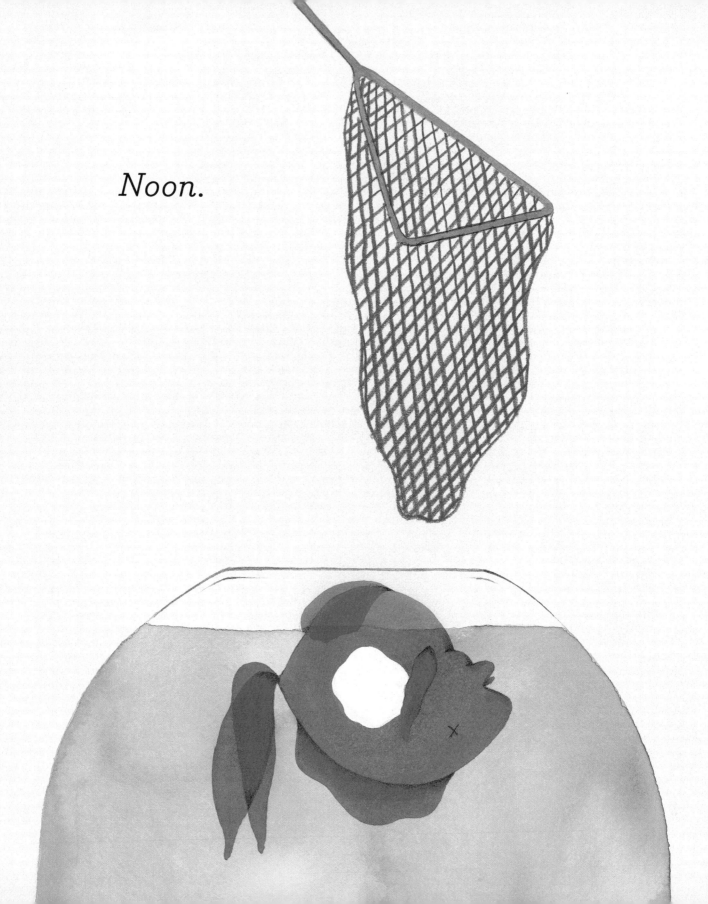

Oh, dear.

After school.

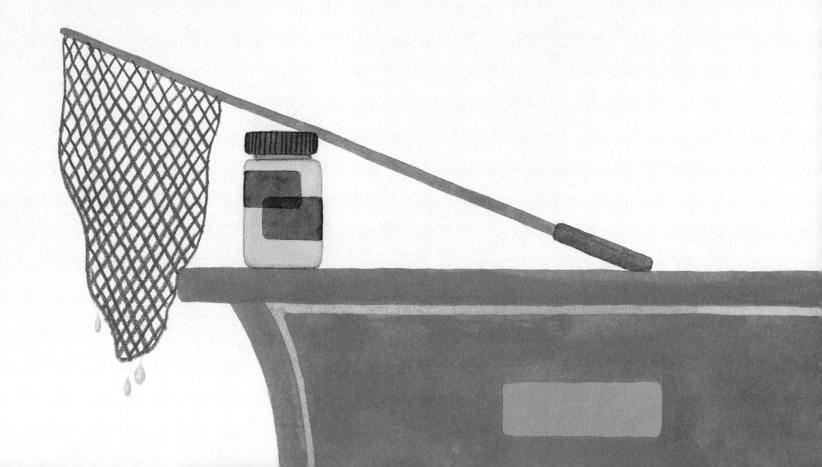

Mom! Splotch ran away!

I have to find him!

LOST FISH!
"SPLOTH"
Orange-1 Splotch
call
495
REWARD
Friendly gold Fish
Answers to Splotch
HAVE YOU SEEN MY SPLOTCH?
Please put in
water and
URGENT
RUN AWAY GOLD FISH!
Please Help!
Very Friendly
likes Food
and water
Call Jefrey

Don't worry, honey.
I'm sure that Splotch
will come home soon.

Next day. After school.

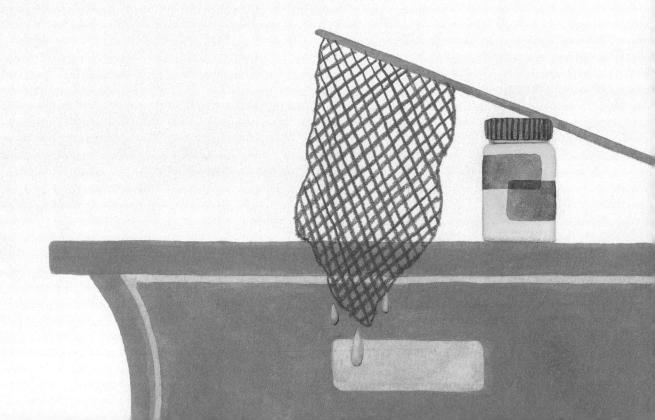

Mom! Splotch is back!

Midnight.

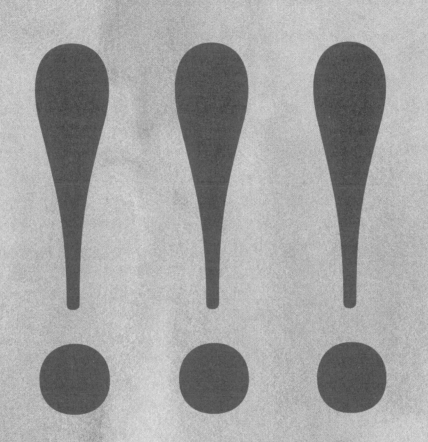

MOM!

Splotch has been
CHANGED
BY ALIENS!!

That's *silly.*
I'm sure Splotch will be back
to normal soon.

Very, very soon.

Next day. After school.

MOM!
Call the police!
This is NOT Splotch!

A few minutes later.

Don't worry, Mom.
We'll find Splotch soon.
Very, very soon.

Don't worry, Splash.
She'll never catch on!

For Gaby

VIKING
Penguin Young Readers Group
An imprint of Penguin Random House LLC
375 Hudson Street, New York, New York 10014

First published in the United States of America by Viking,
an imprint of Penguin Random House LLC, 2017

Copyright © 2017 by Gianna Marino

Penguin supports copyright. Copyright fuels creativity, encourages diverse voices, promotes free speech,
and creates a vibrant culture. Thank you for buying an authorized edition of this book and for complying
with copyright laws by not reproducing, scanning, or distributing any part of it in any form without permission.
You are supporting writers and allowing Penguin to continue to publish books for every reader.

LIBRARY OF CONGRESS CATALOGING-IN-PUBLICATION DATA IS AVAILABLE
ISBN: 9780451469571

Manufactured in China   Set in Bodoni Egyptian Pro   Book design by Nancy Brennan
The illustrations in this book were rendered with gouache and pencil on Fabriano watercolor paper.

1 3 5 7 9 10 8 6 4 2